the Gilded Idol

written by Andrew Whyte ◆ ilustrated by Anna Bron

A great man
is great
by nature.

Superior in form and substance.

He is widely read in those subjects which deserve study.

From frigid north to barren south.

Having
conquered a
hundred summits,
he then conquered
a hundred more...

And this is not to begin to mention his conspicuous success in profession.

With a wealth appropriate in greatness to his character...

He was afforded every opportunity, and each he took...

As he took

this...

The beast was vast and fibrous, sinewy and sleek.

Lead shot
would not
penetrate...

And within a brief rifle flash, before the crack resounded from the tar black jungle walls...

It could leap a hundred paces or more.

However, with net and chain he would not be deprived his prize...

A fit prize that he deserved. A prize which stood then in his manor by the sea.

A fine crypt

in which

you live.

A bestial growling

and nothing

more.

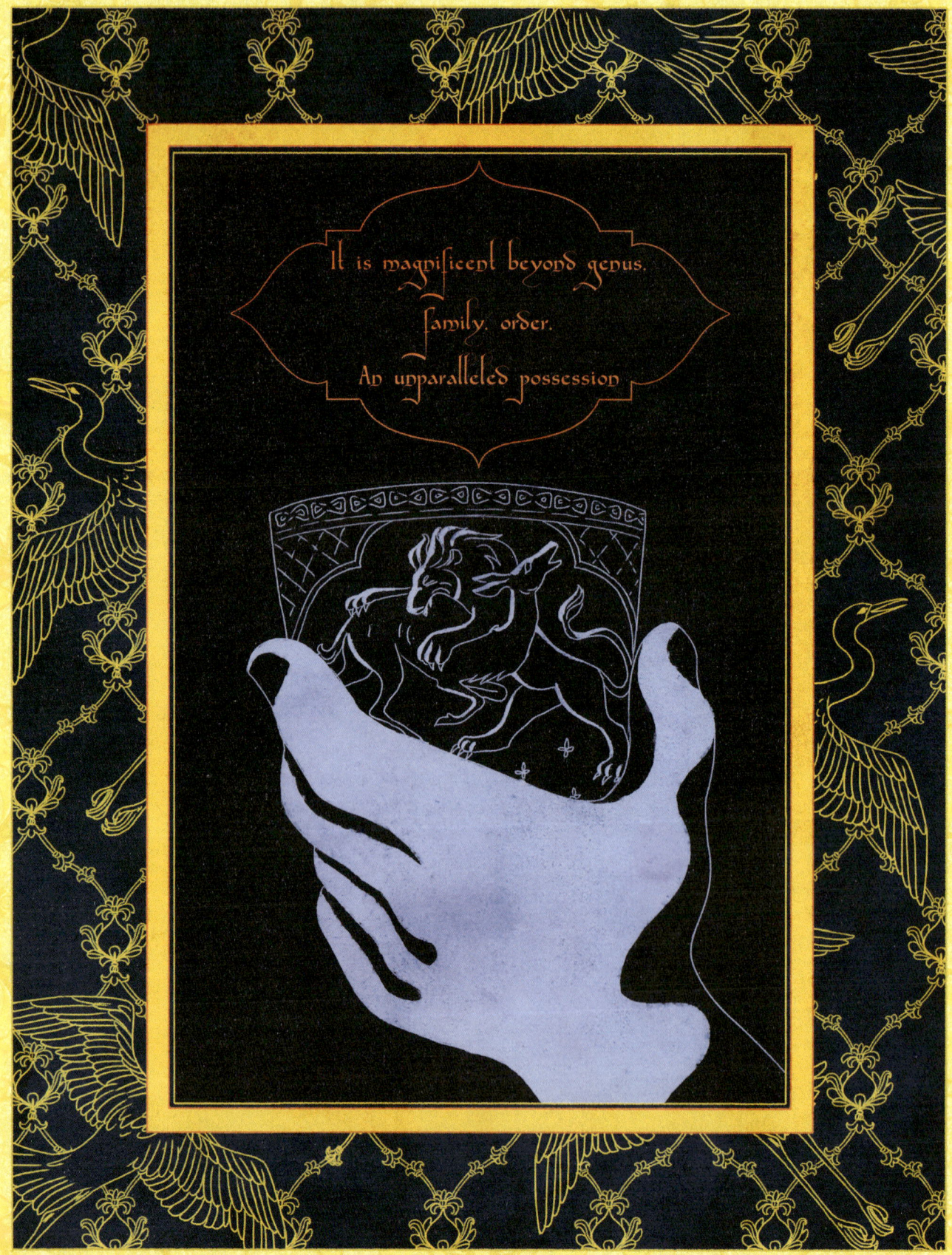

It is magnificent beyond genus.

family. order.

An unparalleled possession

But only a possession.

Out beast!
Hide ye in discordant

jungle, or misty gully and

still will

I find you

out!

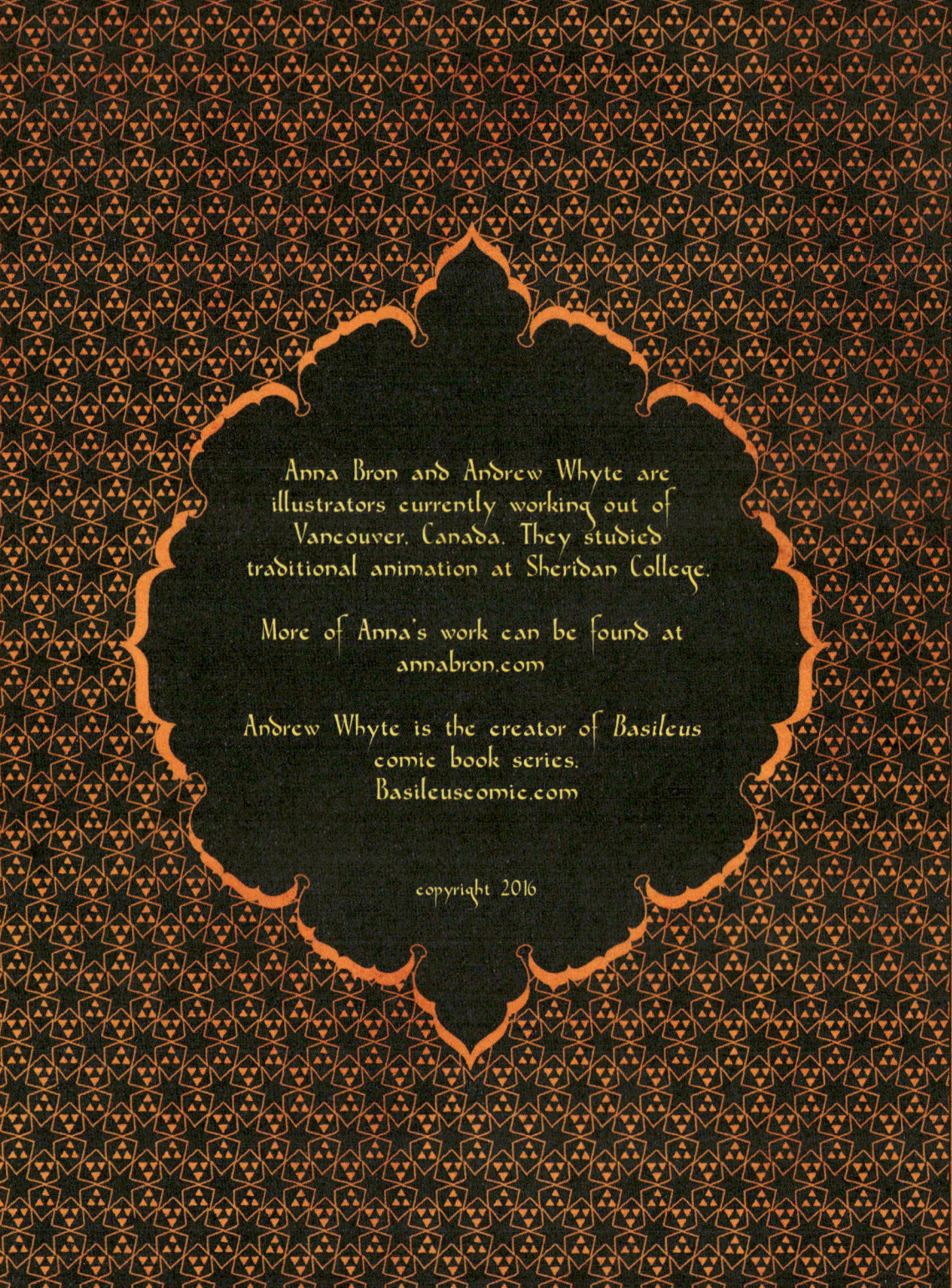

Anna Bron and Andrew Whyte are
illustrators currently working out of
Vancouver, Canada. They studied
traditional animation at Sheridan College.

More of Anna's work can be found at
annabron.com

Andrew Whyte is the creator of *Basileus*
comic book series.
Basileuscomic.com